Tree-House Comix Proudly Presents

DOG MAN
FETCH-22

WRITTEN AND ILLUSTRATED BY **DAV PILKEY**

AS GEORGE BEARD AND HAROLD HUTCHINS

WITH COLOR BY JOSE GARIBALDI

graphix

AN IMPRINT OF

SCHOLASTIC

FOR MY EDITOR
AND FRIEND, KEN GEIST

The term "race car brain with bicycle brakes" on page 35 was coined
by Dr. Edward M. Hallowell, M.D., co-author of Delivered from Distraction:
Getting the Most out of Life with Attention Deficit Disorder.

Library of Congress Control Number 2019944440

978-1-338-32321-4 (POB)
978-1-338-32322-1 (Library)

10 9 8 7 6 5 4 3 2 1   19 20 21 22 23

Printed in China   62
First edition, December 2019

Edited by Ken Geist
Book design by Dav Pilkey and Phil Falco
Color by Jose Garibaldi
Color flatting by Aaron Polk
Publisher: David Saylor

CHAPTERS

INTRO #1: George AND Harold

The Men behind the Dog, Man!

Yo, SNOOPS!!! It's your old Buddies George and Harold! 'sup?

We Just started 6th Grade a few months ago.

My, how Time Flies!

Now that we're GROWN-UPS, we've got some work to do!

So we're cleaning out our tree house.

TRASH

Yep! We're getting rid of all this KID STUFF...

... To make room for GROWN-UP STUFF!

TRASH

While we ~~play with dolls~~ continue our pursuit of extreme Maturity, Please enjoy our Latest foray into Supa-Sophistication.

INTRO #2 DOG MAN

our Story thus Far:

One time a cop and a police dog...

...Got hurt in an explosion!!!

KA-BLAM

wee-ooo-wee-ooo

They got rushed to the Hospital...

...Where the Doctor Gave them the terrible news:

BOO HOO!

Dude! Your Head is **DYING**!!!

Phooey!

And Doggy—Your body is dying!!!

whine whine

ALL Hope is Lost!!!

No it Ain't!

↖ Nurse Lady

Let's stitch the dog's head onto the cop's body!!!

Great idea, nurse lady!

And soon, an awesome new Hero was Born!!!

HOORAY FOR DOG MAN!!!

But then, things got complicated...

Petey the cat was busy living a life of wretchedness...

HAW HAW!

...when he accidentally created a kitty clone.

Papa?

Petey tried to make his little clone become evil...

...but it was not to be.

Kiss

Li'l Petey's kindness melted his Papa's heart...

... and now they are a family.

During the week, Li'l Petey lives with his Papa in a secret laboratory.

They build awesome robots together.

But on the weekends, Li'l Petey lives with his OTHER family.

80-HD: The world's most Remarkable Robot Buddy.

Their House.

Together they play and make comics and stuff...

...but when help is needed, they transform into superheroes!!!

In our last adventure, Petey was Reunited with his Long-Lost father.

It did not go well!

Petey's father stole all of their stuff...

...but he got busted by the cops.

Now he's in the slammer!

THAT'S NOT FAIR!!!

Tree-House Comix Proudly Presents

CHAPTER 1

THE FAIR FAIRY

By George Beard and Harold Hutchins

Hey, fellas!!!

Hey, fellas!!!

The fair fairy's about to start!

Let's Go!!!

RIP!

FLip FLop FLip FLop

16

20

I'm much CALmer Today!

AND STOP CALLING ME "DUDE"!!!!!

whatevs!

Now Let's welcome our first guests, Tim and Brenda.

Tim is angry because Brenda got two toys, and he only got one.

Yeah! IT's NOT FAIR!

Nine Minutes LaTer...

CHAPTER 2

Shared Custody

By George Beard and Harold Hutchins

Soon...

Hey, fellas, it's almost five o'clock!

That means my Papa is gonna come over.

He's going to take me to his house for the week!

Remember our plan?

OK! Let's do it!!!

And so...

OH. Hey, kid!

Hi, Papa!

Are ya ready to go?

Yeah.

I just gotta get my backpack!

31

GET OUT OF THAT BACKPACK RIGHT NOW!

LOOK—WE HAD A DEAL!

You're supposed to live with **ME** during the week...

...And **THOSE GUYS** on the weekends, remember?

Yeah.

Well ya **CAN'T** bring them with you!!!

Rats!

NOW LET'S GO!

Bye, fellas!

Hey, Papa...

...How come Dog Man and 80-HD can't come and stay with us???

Because They **CAN'T!!!**

Why?

Look, I'm not trying to be mean...

...but Dog Man is a— he's just—

He'd lose his own **HEAD** if it wasn't sewn on!

And 80-HD is— he's just—

He's got a **RACE CAR BRAIN** with **BicyCLe BRAKES!**

I just don't want those guys living in **OUR** house!!!

It's not fair!!!

Yeah, well, Life Ain't fair, kid. Get used to it!!!

Poopy-doopy-stoopy-floopy

AND STOP THAT WHINING!!!

Look, Kid. You're RIGHT! It isn't FAIR!

YOU'VE got TWO families who love you...

...And there are some kittens out there who don't even have ONE family!!!

I'll try to be more grateful.

I WAS RIGHT About SOMETHING!

Sweeeeet!!!

CHAPTER 3

The Discovery

By George Beard and Harold Hutchins

The next day...

GASSY Behemoth TeLeVision

STUDIO A

STUDIO B

You wanted to see me, Larry?

MY NAME is SAM!

Whatever.

TAKE A CHAIR!!!

OK. I'll take this one.

HEY! Where DO yA Think you're Going?

"YOU SAID I COULD T... SIT DOWN!"

I'm still keeping the chair, Larry!

Look— we've had **TONS** of complaints about your show!

You're mean to the children, you're rude to the staff...

Flip

...You don't show up to work, you tell lies constantly...

FLIP
FLIP

44

Meanwhile...

What'cha doing, Kid?

I just made a discovery, Papa.

Supa Brain Dots contain a chemical called GR-2.

In high doses, it causes **SUPA ANGER!**

Look! This morning an **ANT** stole one of my Supa Brain Dots...

...and she started eating it.

First she Got Psychokinetic Brain Powers...

YAAAAAAA!

... And she started moving things with her mind.

?

Then came the SUPA Anger!

I'll Get You!!

I drew these FLiP-O-Ramas to show the progression!

the Progressive Stages of SUPA ANGER in FLIP-O-RAMA™

Grrr!

INTRODUCING FLiP-O

STEP 1.
First, place your Left hand inside the dotted Lines marked "Left hand here." Hold the book open FLAT!

STEP 2:
Grasp the right-hand page with your Thumb and index finger (inside the dotted Lines marked "Right Thumb Here").

STEP 3:
Now quickly flip the right-hand page back and forth until the picture appears to be Animated.

(for extra fun, try adding your own sound-effects!)

O-RAMA

REMEMBER,

While you are flipping, be sure you can see the image on page **49** **AND** the image on page **51**.

If you flip quickly, the two pictures will start to look like **ONE** **ANIMATED** cartoon.

Don't forget to add your own sound-effects!!!

Left hand here.

Stage 1
Anger
"Ant vs. Ant"
11:15 AM

Stage 2
Angrier
"Ant vs. Beetle"
11:17 AM

Stage 3
Supa Anger
"Ant vs. Kid with
Magnifying Glass"
11:30 AM

Right
Thumb
here.

But he's **chANGed,** Papa. He's my friend now!

He's even in my comic club. See?

We make comics for each other every day!

I don't want you getting involved with that crazy fish!!!

It's too Late, Papa. I already sent my findings to Sarah!

She's gonna do a news story about it!

SLAP

ALRIGHT, Let's GO!

Where?

I need you to hold the ladder for me.

Why?

Your Grampa stole the Letters from our sign...

...So I'm Gonna put some new Letters up!

Hey! What happened to Grampa?

But he's my Grampa!

HE BETRAYED YOU, TOO!

Trust me! That guy doesn't care about anybody but himself!

But Papa...

WE ARE NOT VISITING YOUR GRAMPA AND THAT IS FINAL!!!

CHAPTER 4
Visiting Grampa

By George Beard AND Harold Hutchins

Hi! I'm Sarah Hatoff with Breaking News!

Sarah Hatoff · LiVE

A DRUG company has recalled all Jars of SuPa Brain Dots ...

TV

But don't worry, folks!

chief

Right now, my most trusted officer...

chief

...is going to every store in the city...

chief

... and collecting all Jars of this dangerous drug!!!

chief

With Dog Man in Charge, what could Possibly go wrong?

really?

Meanwhile...

Roxy's Pharmacy

open

Roxy's Pharmacy

SHAKA SHAKA Shake

CLANK CLANK KLUNK

SHAKA SHAKA Shake

ZOOM

SLAM

GET OUT OF HERE NOW!

Meanwhile...

It's so **UNFAIR!!!**

I can't believe Larry **FiReD** me!

I can!

He shoulda fired you a looooong time ago, dude!

NOBODY ASKED YOU, DOWNWARD DOG!!!

whatevs.

I **MUST** get my **REVENGE!!!**

Mirror, mirror, by the tree...

...Who's the **FAIREST?** Is it **ME**?

Yeah!

WHO SAID THAT?

I did!

Meanwhile...

CAT Jail →

I can't believe you talked me into visiting your Grampa!!!

He's just going to betray us Again!

Maybe he will, Maybe he won't!

But don't you think we should give him another chance?

NO, I DON'T!

And So...

CAT JAIL

Oh, Gramps!!!

WHAT?!!?

HEY!!! What's Going On?

Are you Concocting Some Sort of **Sleep GAS** or something?

Hi, Guys!

Visiting Room

I've missed you so much, Son!

Yeah, **RiGhT!**

And I missed you most of all, Li'L Ralphie!

Li'L Petey!

Yeah! Li'L **PETEY!** That's what I SAID!

Look! I brought you a Present!

Thanks, Grampa!

And I even brought something for **ME!**

CHAPTER 5

TREE-
HOUSE
COMIX
Proudly
Presents

A Buncha Stuff That Happened Next

BY George BEARD 'N' Harold Hutchins

Welcome back to our news show!

And look who's here! It's **DOG MAN!**

He just finished collecting all of the **SUPA BRAIN DOTS** in the city!!!

Now nobody else will develop Psychokinetic Brain Powers...

...**OR** become Supa Angry!

See? I **TOLD** ya nothing would go wrong!!!

Shake a paw, Dog Man!!!

HEY!!!

The WAGON is ROLLING AWAY!

GeT it,
DOG MAN!

POW

PLiP PLiP PLiP PLoP plip PLoP Plippity PLoP PLoP plip plop Pli

Glug Glug Glug

SQUIRCH

And now for the finishing touch!!!

83

OH, GUARD!

Yes, Petey?

My Dad just fell asleep!

Oh, dear! I'd better get him into bed!

cat JAIL

And so...

Meanwhile...

What's happening to us ???

My brain feels weird.

Mine too!!!

It's almost as if we've all developed psycho-kinetic brain powers somehow!!!

Yeah!

But how could such a thing have happened?

Beats me!

HEY!

Left hand here.

Right
Thumb
here.

STOP!

How did this **TREE** come to **LIFE**???

We're controlling it with our minds!

Yeah! We're **SUPA Angry!**

And we're not gonna let you leave us AGAIN!!!!!!!

Now, Now — wait just a minute!

Maybe we can all work something out!

CHAPTER 6
BARKY McTreeFace

Down to the city...

...causing Cataclysmic crime...

Right
Thumb
here.

Flippity Flip-Flip
Slappity-slap.
Look at Barky Punch!
Flippity Flip-Flip
Kickety-Kick.
He'll eat ya up for Lunch!

Haw Haw Haw! Look at that **DESTRUCTION!**

Now things Are becoming **FAIR!**

Wait a minute— How does **THiS** Make things Fair?

I Just lost my **JoB!** I Lost **EVERYTHING!**

Yeah. So?

So now I'm taking **EVERYTHiNG** Away from **EVERYoNE** else!

109

Meanwhile...

HEY!!!

What's the big idea?

You fell asleep, Grampa!

GRAMPA?

I'm **NOT GRAMPA!** I'm <u>PETEY</u>!!!!!

Yeah, but what about your tail and whiskers???

That's just **GLUE** and **MARKERS** and stuff!!!

Sorry, Grampa! I'm not falling for your tricks AGain!

WAit A minute—I've Gotta find my SoN!

Oh, don't worry about him...

...Petey left here about an hour ago.

He had your little Grandson with him!

LOOK-You've got to Listen to Me!

THAT KID is in TERRIBLE DANGER! LET ME OUT OF HERE NOW!!!

Hi, Grampa!

Okay.

Hey, I'm Hungry!

Well go cook some food then, ya freeloader!

What do I look like? Your **SERVANT?**

My Papa always cooks for me.

You **DID** say you were my Papa, didn't you?

SLAP!

And so...

Later...

PETEY & SON

Hey, Papa!

What Now?

More Popcorn, please.

I'm **NOT** MAKING ANY MORE POPCORN!

But my Papa ALWAYS makes more popcorn!

You **DID** say you were my Papa, didn't you?

THAT KID IS DRIVING Me CRAZY!

POP POP POP POP POP POP POP POP POP

CHAPTER 7

FLIPPY RETURNS

Meanwhile...

FISH JaiL

FiSh JaiL

Haw Haw Haw Haw!

ish aiL

MY evil PLan is WORKinG!!!!!!!

Soon I shall take over the World!!!

But first, I must destroy that Robo-cat!

HAW HAW HAW

HAW HAW HAW

What happened next, Flippy?

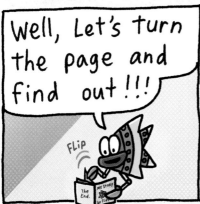

Well, Let's turn the page and find out!!!

FLiP

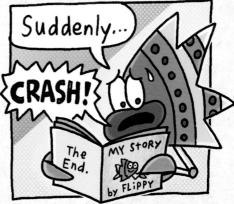

Suddenly...

CRASH!

The End.

MY STORY by FLiPPY

...The Robo-cat was in my Grasp!!!

The end.

Hooray! Awesome!

Sweeet!

CAT KID'S COMIC CLUB

YAY! Bravo!!! Thanks, everyone!!!

But then...

Hey, FLIPPY! the Mayor's on the phone!

Hello?

Pack your bags, FLIPPY! You're a FREE FISH!

I am?

Yep! Li'L Petey's Research Proved you were innocent!!!

...Twenty-Two tiny Tadpoles!!!

They all have Psychokinetic Powers...

...And they all seem SUPA ANGRY!

Gee — I wonder how THAT HAPPENED!

Well, uh, he was—

And DON'T BLAME DOG Man! It WAS Your FauLt, too!!!

...Well, uh...

...MISTAKES were MADE!!!

But don't worry, Folks! I've put Dog Man in charge...

...of fetching those twenty-two tiny Tadpoles!!!

Once he fetches them...

...we'll get them the help they need!

See? With DOG
Man in charge...

...What could...
uh, Possibly...

...g- go wrong?

YOU BETTER
GO HELP him!

Well, uh — Okay...

...But who's gonna
Help **me**?

Well, Zuzu, I guess it's up to us !!!

Let's GO SAVE The world Again!

Oh, boy, this is Gonna be **GREAT!!!**

CHAPTER 8

The Fetcher in the Sky

Meanwhile...

Cat Jail

I'm so glad we're roommates, Grampa!

I'm NOT GRAMPA! I Already told ya, like, A MILLiON TiMES!

I know. And I believe you, Grampa!

🎵 Beep!

But then...

We interrupt this tenderhearted moment with Breaking News:

Dog Man and chief are heading to town...

...to stop the evil tree that is ATTACKING the city!

EviL Tree? Attacking the city?

This looks like a job for **COMMANDER CUPCAKE!!!**

Huff Puff Huff

Huff Puff Puff

...And I champion the cause of carbohydrates!

Amen!

NOBODY CARES!!!

But--- But I'm Commander Cupcake!

WELL THAT'S JUST GREAT!

I was just thinking: what we **REALLY NEED** Right Now...

...is A Guy in a Cape whose **ONLY** Superpower is that he eats a lot of **CUPCAKES!!!**

I also eat sprinkles!

THAT'S NOT HELPFUL!!!

YOU HAD AN ESCAPE TUNNEL THIS WHOLE TIME...

...AND YOU DIDN'T TELL ME??

You didn't ask!

Meanwhile...

As Dog Man and his friends got closer to the scene of the crime...

... they Grabbed some weapons...

... and Prepared for an epic Battle!!!

It's time to give up, Fair Fairy!!!

NEVER!!! You **DO-GOODERS** can't stop my **SUPA-AnGRY PSYCHOKineTic TADPoLes!**

STOP The TADpoles, DOG Man!!!

STOP The Dog Man, Tadpoles!!!

Left hand here.

And so...

HEY!!!

Zip

DUDE! That Poodle is Getting away!!!

Aw, Let her go!

She's just a tiny Poodle.

What could one tiny Poodle Possibly do?

CHAPTER 9

Run, Zuzu, Run!!

Peter
&
son

You did, too!!!

I DiD **NOT**!

Oh, hi, Zuzu!

Screech

BARK BARK BARK!!!

What's that you say? DoG Man's in trouble?

Ruff Ruff BARK BARK BARK!

Sarah and Chief, too?

BARK BARK GRRR OWOOOOOOOooo!

Unspeakable evil? Mindless chaos ???

Unlimited supa powers with no moral compass?

This looks like a job for the SUPA BUDDIES!

C'mon, Zuzu!

slide

Meanwhile...

Well, here we are at last, Grampa...

...MY Cupcake Command Center.™

Let's check the cupcake computer!

Click-clack-clickity clack-Beep-Boop...

COMPYUDUH. cupcakes. YUM Eat it.

Hey! That's not a real keyboard!

It's just a Pizza box with stuff drawn on it!!!

...And ya spelled "Computer" wrong!!!

COMPYUDUH. cupcakes. YUM Eat it.

Look, We need to Get out of Here!!!

TO THE CUPCAKEMOBILE!

Behold: The Latest in Cupcake Technology!!!

I just need to glue on the last paper plate...

...I mean "TIRE"!

PBBBBBT

Uh-oh...

Look, we haven't got time for this!

I've gotta go and save my SON!!!

But you haven't seen the cupcake cabana yet...

...Or the cupcake croquet court...

...or the—

I JUST WANNA SEE THE CUPCAKE EXIT!!!

Atomic Cupcake Powers Activate.

PBBBBBT!

CUPCAKE Exit ↓

PBBBBBBBBT!!!

PBBPBBBBPBBBBT

CUPCAKE entrance ↘

CHAPTER 10
MY FAIR LADY

Hello again, folks! I'm Sarah Hatoff Reporting from...

..a floating net.

We've all been captured by twenty-two Supa-angry psychokinetic tadpoles...

...And they're holding us in the sky with their Brain Powers.

How will we ever get out of this mess???

BUMP BINK BOMP

Gee, that was a lot easier than I thought it would be!!!

And Look, Flippy the bionic Butterfly fish...

...has joined our fight for **GOOD!**

We must eat that Gigantic cupcake!

It's not **REAL**, ya know!

Only then can we Save the world!!!

It's just a **SIGN!!!**

Almost there...

Meanwhile...

HUFF PUFF HUFF

At Last I've found You!

Who the heck are **YOU**?

Allow me to introduce myself!

I'm your **NEW** PARTNER in Crime!

PARTNER? What do I need a PARTNER for?

Can't You see I'm Just about to DeFeAt the SuPA Buddies?

Indeed she was Right. The Supa Buddies and their friends...

...had Given their all...

...and had put up a valiant fight.

(GooD Vibes)

But they were outnumbered...

CRASH!

... outmatched...

... and out of time!

One by one, our heroes were captured...

...And the powers of evil grew stronger and stronger.

Look at me!!! I'm **FLYING**, BABY!

CHAPTER 11

The Cat Kid Conundrum

174

Ready to slice.

And in this perfect moment...

...When a swipe from his sharpened sabers...

...Promises sweet salvation...

... he stops.

ShinG

HEY!

I didn't see ya back there.

You could have clobbered me!

I know.

You could have sliced us all into sushi.

I know.

You could have saved all of your friends.

I know.

But you didn't.

What's Your name?

Molly.

Oh. I'm Li'l Petey.

Hey, guess what? I have a comic club!

You do?

Yeah. You can join if you want to.

But I never made a comic before.

It's okay.

I can show ya how. It's FUN!!!

You'll teach me?

of course.

That's what friends do. They help each other.

As the two friends talked and laughed, something started to change in Molly...

Ha Ha Ha

Ha Ha Ha

... and soon, her Supa Anger began melting away.

WHAT'S GOING ON HERE?!!?

Mommy, this is Li'l Petey!

He's my FRIEND!

NO HE'S NOT!!! He's YOUR ENEMY!

But, Mommy, I think—

YOU'RE NOT SUPPOSED to THINK!!

YOU'RE SUPPOSED TO OBEY!

CHAPTER 12
Good Golly Miss Molly

It is easy to join with the crowd...

...and even easier to spread anger and hate.

But it takes courage to stand alone.

And kindness often takes the most courage of all.

Molly could not move the mighty tree all by herself...

...but she could move a branch...

C-C-CREAK!

...and that was all she needed.

C'mon, gang! I've got an idea!!!

They're Getting Away!!!

Aw, Let 'em Go!

What could one tiny tadpole and one tiny kitten and one tiny poodle possibly do?

DUDE— seriously?

Hey, what's up, 'Puter?

'Sup?

supa 'puter

We need your help, brah!

'K

We need to create an **ANTiDOTE** to Supa Brain Dots.

No prob. I'll download the components...

...then calculate a recipe for our concoction using everyday ingredients.

Sweeet!

C'mon, gang! Let's go find some everyday ingredients!!!

And soon...

Ok, what next?

...now add two teaspoons of ketchup...

...and a dash of paprika...

Lastly, pour the mixture into my subcritical fission reactor.

One Nuclear transmutation Later...

Soon...

Hi, Papa!

Where have **YOU** been?

Those Tadpoles are almost done destroying your friends!

We were making an **ANTIDOTE!!!**

It's in this balloon!

All we have to do is pop it...

...and those tadpoles will all lose their SUPA Powers!!!!!

You better go hide in that swamp now, Molly...

...and stay under the water so ya won't breathe the antidote!

That way You won't lose **YOUR** Supa Powers!!!

Okay! See ya later!!!

OK, TADPOLES— LISTEN UP!!!!

I want You all to hide in that SWAMP over there!

StaY Underwater, and don't breathe the air for a few minutes!!!

OK, Mommy!

See Ya Later!

Bye, Mom!

Mean-while...

You'd better wipe that **SMILE** off of Your face, Young Lady...

...because things are about to Get **SERIOUS!!!**

He's Gonna Pop that balloon and...

...and...

THAT ANTIDOTE RUINED EVERYTHING!

Hey, wait a minute!

THERE'S No Antidote in this balloon, is there???

Nope.

YOU LIED TO ME!!! YOU BETRAYED ME!!

I guess I did...

... **GRAMPA!**

Zuzu's the real hero Today!!!

She poured the antidote into the swamp and saved the world!!!

HOORAY FOR ZUZU!!!

whisper whisper whisper

CRASH!

Hey, Look! Commander Cupcake did it **AGAIN!**

He captured the Fair Fairy _AND_ Grampa!!!

You two criminals are Going to **JAiL!**

Left hand here.

Gentle Rinse

Delicate cleanse

Relaxing Blow Dry

Right Thumb here.

Chapter 14

Do Good, Flippy

Alright, let's Go, kid!

Hey, Papa, Flippy and Molly don't have anywhere to Live.

Can they stay with us for a while?

Pleeease?

Please? Please? Please? Please? Please? Please? Please? Please? Please? Supa-Dupa Please?

Well, okay. But only for a

YAY!

Where, Flippy?

Well, there are twenty-one baby tadpoles in that swamp back there...

...and I'll bet they're feeling pretty lonely and afraid all by themselves.

I remember how that felt.

So I was thinking...

217

...maybe they could use a friend.

You were so good to me when I was in fish jail, L.P.

You made comics for me every day!

You inspired me! You kept me going!

Now it's my turn to **DO GOOD!**

Hey! I wanna do good, too!!!

Well you can help me if ya want!

Okay!

And you guys can visit us at the swamp anytime!!!

Yeah! You still have to teach me how to make comics!

I will!

Maybe you can teach all twenty-two of us!

Okay!

Well, let's go, kiddo!

Bye, Li'l Petey!

Bye, old guy!

And so...

See, Papa?

I **TOLD** Ya Flippy was a Good Guy!

Yeah. I guess so.

He's changing the world!

Well, I don't Know about <u>that</u>!

I mean, come on!

Maybe You're right, Kid.

I am?

I was **RIGHT** about something?

I said **MAYBE**!

I WAS RIGHT About SomeThing!

FORMER FISH FELON FINDS FAMILY

Flippy the bionic psychokinetic butterfly fish was released from fish jail last week, and is already making an impact in our community. In this exclusive interview, Flippy shares his inspiring story:

Q. How has life changed since you were in Fish Jail?
A. WELL, I MOVED INTO A SWAMP AND NOW I'M RAISING A BUNCH OF BABY TADPOLES.

Q. How did you meet them?
A. WE MET LAST WEEK WHEN THEY TRIED TO DESTROY THE PLANET.

Q. Weren't you afraid of them?
A. NAH. I KNEW THEY WERE GOOD KIDS DEEP DOWN INSIDE. AND I WAS RIGHT.

Q. Were they happy to see you?
A. THEY DIDN'T RECOGNIZE ME. THEY HAD NO MEMORY OF THEIR TERRIFYING ORDEAL. IN FACT, THEY ALL STARTED CALLING ME "DADDY."

Menu   ☰

Q. So what did you do?
A. I HAD NO CHOICE. I ADOPTED THEM ALL.
Q. So what's next for you and your new family?
A. RIGHT NOW I'M TEACHING EVERYBODY TO READ AND WRITE. MY FRIEND MOLLY IS HELPING, AND CAT KID IS TEACHING US ALL HOW TO MAKE OUR OWN COMICS!

CAT KID'S COMIC CLUB!

Local kitten Li'l Petey has started his own comic club, and it's gaining new members every day. If you would like to start your OWN chapter of Cat Kid's Comic Club, go to scholastic.com/catkidclub to download everything you need. It's free and it's FUN!

DOG MAN IS GO!

An ALL-NEW Dog Man novel is coming SOON, and it's going to be the BEST ONE YET!!! The title of the all-
graphic novel is going to be DOG MAN
it will be available next sum

by George and Harold

⭐ On pages 6 and 7, George is adapting a well-known quote from the Bible. (1 Corinthians 13:11 (KJV & NLT).)

⭐ Petey's rant on page 36-38 was inspired by the following Quote:

> "Life is never fair... And perhaps
> it is a good thing for most of us
> that it is not." — Oscar Wilde

⭐ The Barky McTreeface song (Chapter 6) can be sung to the tune of any magical snowman-themed song you can think of.

⭐ The final chapter was inspired by <u>The Star Thrower</u> by Loren Eiseley, as well as Joel Barker's adaptation. It goes kinda like this:

> A guy walking along the seashore
> saw a kid picking up starfish from the sand
> and gently throwing them back into the ocean.
> "Whatcha doing?" asked the guy.
> "These starfish were washed ashore," said the kid,
> "and they will die if they don't get back to the sea."
> "But there are thousands of starfish along this shore,"
> said the guy. "You can't possibly make a difference."
> The kid gently threw another starfish out into the sea.
> "I made a difference to that one," she said.

in **29** Ridiculously easy steps!

229

HOW 2 DRAW Li'L PeTeY

in **21** Ridiculously Easy steps!

MOLLY

in 9 Ridiculously Easy Steps!

① ② ③ ④ ⑤ ⑥

⑦

⑧

⑨

233

BONUS!

NOW YOU CAN SING THE FINAL VERSES OF BARKY'S SONG!

Oh, Barky McTreeface
Knew the moon was bright that night.
So he grabbed his foes with his hands and toes
And he squeezed them really tight!

Then all the tadpoles
flew into a swampy bay.
And the medicine Zuzu poured Right in
Made their powers go away!

So Barky dropped our heroes
and he turned back to a tree.
Then the bad guys went to jail and
that's the end of our story.

Now Barky McTreeface
is so peaceful, calm, and zen.
And if you do good like ya know you should
then he won't come back again!!!

Peace-ity peace-peace, zen-ity zen
Look at Barky now!
Do-ity Do-Do, Good-ity Good
He won't come back No-how!!!

YOU BETTER NOT!

OLD LADY JAIL

LEARN 2 DRAW MORE STUFF!

at Scholastic.com and Pilkey.com

GET READING W

— But I'm ~~un~~der cupcake!

WELL THAT'S JUST GREAT!

~~w~~as just thinking: ~~th~~at we **REALLY** ~~n~~**EED** Right Now...

...is A Guy in a Cape whose **ONLY** Superpower is that he eats a lot of **CUPCAKES!!!**

I also eat sprinkles!

THAT'S NOT HELPFUL!!!

ABOUT THE AUTHOR-ILLUSTRATOR

When Dav Pilkey was a kid, he was diagnosed with ADHD and dyslexia. Dav was so disruptive in class that his teachers made him sit out in the hall every day. Luckily, Dav loved to draw and make up stories. He spent his time in the hallway creating his own original comic books.

In the second grade, Dav Pilkey made a comic book about a superhero named Captain Underpants. Since then, he has been creating books that explore fun, positive themes and inspire readers everywhere.

ABOUT THE COLORIST

Jose Garibaldi grew up on the South Side of Chicago. As a kid, he was a daydreamer and a doodler, and now it's his full-time job to do both. Jose is a professional illustrator, painter, and cartoonist who has created work for many organizations, including Nickelodeon, MAD Magazine, Cartoon Network, Disney, and THE EPIC ADVENTURES OF CAPTAIN UNDERPANTS for DreamWorks Animation. He lives in Los Angeles, California, with his wonder dogs, Herman and Spanky.

ITH DAV PILKEY!

ABOUT THE AUTHOR-ILLUSTRATOR

When Dav Pilkey was a kid, he was diagnosed with ADHD and dyslexia. Dav was so disruptive in class that his teachers made him sit out in the hall every day. Luckily, Dav loved to draw and make up stories. He spent his time in the hallway creating his own original comic books.

In the second grade, Dav Pilkey made a comic book about a superhero named Captain Underpants. Since then, he has been creating books that explore fun, positive themes and inspire readers everywhere.

ABOUT THE COLORIST

Jose Garibaldi grew up on the South Side of Chicago. As a kid, he was a daydreamer and a doodler, and now it's his full-time job to do both. Jose is a professional illustrator, painter, and cartoonist who has created work for many organizations, including Nickelodeon, MAD Magazine, Cartoon Network, Disney, and THE EPIC ADVENTURES OF CAPTAIN UNDERPANTS for DreamWorks Animation. He lives in Los Angeles, California, with his wonder dogs, Herman and Spanky.

But--- But I'm Commander cupcake!

WeLL THAT'S JUST GReAT!

I was just thinking: What we **REALLY NEED** Right Now...

...is A Guy in a Cape whose **ONLY** Superpower is that he eats a lot of **CUPCAKES!!!**

I also eat sprinkles!

THAT'S NOT HeLPFUL!!!